COOKING WITH HERB
The Vegetarian Dragon

Grand-Pa-Pa-Snap-Dragon

Grand-Ma-Ma-Flora

Herb

For Jeannine, who loves me and my cooking — J. B.
For Penny, Paul, Charles, Sara, Alex and Kate — D. H.

Barefoot Books
37 West 17th Street, 4th Floor East
New York, New York 10011

This book was typeset in Flareserif and Helvetica, and printed on 100% acid-free paper
The illustrations were prepared in watercolor, crayon, pen and ink on thick watercolor paper

Graphic design by Tom Grzelinski, England. Color separation by Grafiscan, Italy
Printed and bound in Singapore by Tien Wah Press (Pte) Ltd

1 3 5 7 9 8 6 4 2

Publisher Cataloging-in-Publication Data

Bass, Jules.
   Cooking with Herb, the vegetarian dragon : a cookbook for
kids / written by Jules Bass ; illustrated by Debbie Harter.—1st ed.
[40]p. : col. ill. ;   cm.
Summary: A hilarious cookbook, ideal for use at home and in the
classroom to introduce children to simple vegetarian cookery.
Herb's tasty and nutritious recipes are complemented with witty
and bright illustrations.
ISBN 1-84148-041-X
1. Cookery—Vegetables—Juvenile literature. 2. Vegetarian
cookery—Juvenile literature. I.Harter, Debbie, ill. II. Title.
641.5/ 636--dc21   1999   AC   CIP

Children should not use this cookbook without
adult supervision.

Neither the publisher nor the author can assume
responsibility for any accident, injuries, losses or
other damages resulting from use of the book.

Haggis

Hopper

Squat

COOKING WITH HERB
The Vegetarian Dragon
A Cookbook for Kids

Rosie-Rose

Meathook

Gorse

Text and recipes by
JULES BASS

Illustrations by
DEBBIE HARTER

Barefoot Books

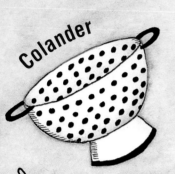
Colander

Stockpot

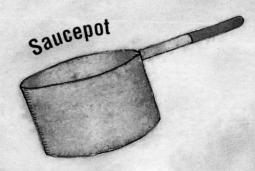
Saucepot

Sieve

Garlic Press

CONTENTS

Measuring Spoons

Measuring Cups

Grater

Peeler

Blender & Processor

Electric Beater

Measuring Glass

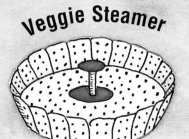
Veggie Steamer

Frypan

Sauté Pan

Ladle

Whisk

Wooden Spoon

Spatula

Cooks' Knives

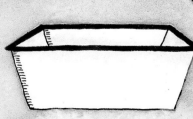
Flipper

Baking Tray

Pastry Cutters

Loaf Pan

Introduction

The recipes in this book are mainly for those I like to call **LOVE** children: **L**=lacto **O**=ova **V**=veggie **E**=eaters. This type of vegetarian diet is reasonable, well accepted and proven to be healthy for kids as well as for dragons like me.

My human friends tell me that The American Academy of Pediatrics, The National Academy of Sciences and The American Medical Association have all sanctioned the lacto-ova vegetarian diet.

A vegetarian could be described as someone who does not eat meat. Sometimes people call themselves vegetarians, but they eat fish. My philosophy is: whatever works. Kids who are thinking about becoming vegetarians don't have to do it overnight. They can take their time — get used to it, however long it takes.

Life isn't a race or a contest. On the way you may fall off the track *and even eat a piece of you-know-what!* No big deal! That doesn't make you a carnivore. And, about your friends who don't want to be vegetarians? Hey, live and let live. Don't make them feel bad about it — and I hope they won't give you a hard time about how *you* want to eat!

A word about the recipes: some kids will be able to prepare them by themselves while others will need some help. Either way I hope you kids *get involved* because cooking can be lots of fun. You get to eat what you've cooked-up. And wait until the first time you hear someone say: "Hey, did you really make this? It tastes great!" It'll make you turn the page and try another of my recipes.

Remember, the recipes aren't just for kids — everyone can join in. Don't forget to let me know how your meal turns out.

Herb

How I Learned to Cook

My Grand-Ma-Ma-Flora was the best cook in our family — sorry, Mom! She gave me my first cooking lesson when I was six years old.

My cousin, Rosie-Rose, and my best dragon-pal, Gorse, were at the lair for lunch that day. We were going to make her famous *spaghetti sandwiches*. I could scarf down a dozen of them and was dying to learn how to make them for myself.

"Now, dragon-littles, before we begin," Grand-Ma-Ma-Flora said, "you'll have to learn how to get everything you're going to cook with ready before you start. That's called 'preparation.' So, let's find all of the ingredients — the foodstuffs you see in the recipe — and all the pots, pans and gadgets, so they'll be handy. Each one has a special use. *Can't boil spaghetti in a frypan, you know!* Just remember: good cooks, like good workers, always use the right tools.

"Now, before we start, there are some safety rules:

1. Never try to catch a falling knife. You could cut yourself. Let it drop.
2. Always keep your knives *sharp* — a sharp knife doesn't slip.
3. Don't press hard on the knife until it's buried in what you're cutting.
4. Always keep your hands *super-dry* so nothing slips.
5. Always wear oven mitts when taking hot stuff out of the oven.
6. DON'T EVER RUSH — that's when you can hurt yourself.
7. Cook with the most important ingredient of all: LOVE!"

Grand-Ma-Ma-Flora took down a mess of utensils from her shelves and handed them out. I got a round metal bowl full of holes. *Whatever would we use that for?* I thought.

"It's a *colander*," said Grand-Ma-Ma-Flora, "and it's used for draining water — like separating the spaghetti from the water you boiled it in."

That sounded like fun! So I gave it a try.

Oh I get it, like this!

I don't think so!

Boy dragons can't learn to cook.

Not if they don't pay attention!
Turn the page.

MY FIRST COOKING LESSON

Because of what Rosie-Rose said about boy dragons not being able to cook, I was determined to show her I could cook with the best of them. This *Spaghetti Sandwich* was the first thing I ever tried to make, and it turned out delicious. It's still one of my favorite recipes. Don't brag about how easy it is. Let your friends think it's really hard to do!

I can say it in Italian, "Free ta ta!"

Grand-Ma-Ma-Flora's ^hard to make^ Spaghetti Sandwich

▾ Here's what you'll have to hunt up: (Serves 2)

About 1 cup (250ml) leftover cold spaghetti (with the sauce mixed in it)
2 tablespoons good olive oil
2 whole eggs, beaten with salt and pepper

¼ cup (50ml) grated Parmesan cheese
Sandwich bread and butter (or substitute)

Preparation time: 15 minutes   *Cooking time*: 10 minutes

1 Turn on the oven broiler to high. Put the rack about 4" (10cm) from the heat.

2 Put the olive oil in a non-stick frypan on medium heat. Add the leftover spaghetti. Turn with a wooden spoon until the spaghetti is warmed.

3 Pour on the eggs and cook for 30 seconds. Sprinkle the cheese over and slide the pan under the broiler.

4 Broil until the eggs are firm and the *frittata* is lightly browned on top. Slide out onto a plate.

To Serve Pile a few slices of the *frittata* on your favourite bread. You've done it! A first-class *spaghetti sandwich*.

* pronounced free-ta-ta which is what this dish is called in Italian.

Herb's Hot Tips

Leave the door of the oven open so that the handle of the frypan sticks out. Be sure to pick it up with an oven mitt.

Grand-Pa-Pa was known as The Grand Snap-Dragon. Maybe that's because he was head of our dragon-clan, or maybe it's because he did tend to snap at dragon-folk. Now G.S. (as he was known to his friends), was a very fussy eater, so the first time he came to lunch I was a nervous wreck. I had decided to try out a new sauce for pasta (G.S. loved his pasta).

Pasta & Sauce for a Grand Snap-Dragon

➤ Here's what you'll have to hunt up: (Serves 4)

1 lb (500gms) pasta (macaroni or penne)
6 tablespoons butter
1 tablespoon flour
Pinch of nutmeg or allspice
½ cup plain bread crumbs

1 ½ cups (360ml) light cream
1 cup (240ml) grated Parmesan cheese
Salt and pepper (to taste)

Preparation time: 10 minutes

Cooking time: 50 minutes

1 Melt the butter in a saucepot on a *very* low heat. Then add the flour and nutmeg and cook for 5 minutes. Stir from time to time with a whisk.

2 Add salt, pepper and the cream. Cook for 10 minutes, whisking from time to time (don't let it burn!) Then put the lid on the saucepot and take off the heat.

3 Pre-heat oven to 450˚F (230˚C; Gas #8). Bring a large spaghetti-pot of water to a boil, add a tablespoon of salt and throw in the pasta. Boil until firm to the tooth - we call that *al dente*: (al-<u>den</u>-tay) in Italian.

4 Warm up the sauce. Put the pasta in a baking dish and pour ²/₃ of the sauce and half of the cheese over it. Mix well. Pour the rest of the sauce on top and sprinkle with the remaining Parmesan and bread crumbs. Bake for 10 minutes.

To Serve Put the baking dish on the table (on a warmer or a trivet) and spoon onto warmed plates.

Hurry it up Herbie, dinner's already 2 minutes late!

G.S's Hot Tips

If the sauce looks too thick, thin it down with some milk. It gets thicker as you cook it.

ROSIE-ROSE BAKES HER FIRST BREAD

When Grand-Ma-Ma-Flora said, "Today, we'll make a pan-bread," Gorse and I said, "No way. Too difficult." Only Rosie-Rose agreed to try. Well, when it was done, we felt silly — it looked so easy. Not only that, the smell of fresh bread attracted a crowd, and I didn't even get a taste. "Serves you right," said Rosie-Rose, "for not trying." So I dumped some flour in a bowl and gave it a try. It really was easy! Now, I bake it all the time.

Rosemary Pan Bread

Look what I've made!

▸ Here's what you'll have to hunt up: (Serves 4)

3 cups (750ml) all-purpose flour
1 teaspoon salt
3 teaspoons dried yeast granules (or 1oz / 8gms compressed yeast)

$^1/_2$ teaspoon sugar
7 tablespoons olive oil
1 cup (250ml) warm water ("baby bottle" warm)
2 tablespoons chopped rosemary

Preparation time: 90 minutes

Cooking time: 15 minutes

1 Put the yeast and sugar in the water and stir until it dissolves. Let it sit for 5 minutes.

2 Combine the flour and salt in a mixer or food processor (with a steel blade). Add 2 tablespoons of olive oil to the water. Turn on the machine and slowly add the water mix to the flour. Stop the moment it forms a ball. Scrape it onto a floured surface and knead with floured hands until smooth (about 5 minutes or more).

3 Allow the ball of dough to rest in a bowl, covered with plastic wrap until it doubles in size (30-40 minutes).

4 Take the dough out of the bowl and punch it down — but

don't knead it. Put it in the center of an oiled baking pan about 9" x 12" x $^3/_4$"(23cm x 30cm x $1^1/_2$cm). Cover with a dishtowel.

5 Pre-heat the oven to 375°F (190°C; Gas #5). After ten minutes, roll (or press out) the dough until it almost covers the bottom of the pan (neatness does *not* count here!) Cover with the towel and let it rest for 10 minutes.

6 Paint the dough with olive oil, sprinkle on the rosemary and extra salt and bake until golden (about 15 minutes).

To Serve Cool on a rack. Slice into squares. Eat while it's warm.

Rosie's Hot Tip

If the dough is too sticky, add a bit of flour. If it's too dry, add a bit of water until it's right.

I remember how we tricked Meathook into eating my famous chili. "How can you make chili without meat?" he bellowed. "It's Chili CON Carne, right? Even I know that 'CON carne' in Spanish means 'WITH meat.' You won't fool me with this one." Then he said he liked it hot, so I added an extra scoop of chili powder. I'm telling you, it was **flame-out hot** — and, of course, meat-less, but he never knew the difference!

Herb's Chili Con "No" Carne

▸ Here's what you'll have to hunt up: (Serves 4)

2 cups (500ml) textured vegetable protein (TVP)
2 cups (500ml) vegetable stock
1 large onion, chopped
2 garlic cloves, pressed
1 small can (350ml) tomatoes, chopped
2 tablespoons cumin powder

$^2/_3$ cup (160ml) red pinto beans (drained)
1 teaspoon dried oregano
2 tablespoons canola or olive oil
Chili powder (to taste)
Salt and pepper (to taste)
Grated cheese, to garnish

Preparation time: 15 minutes

Cooking time: 25 minutes

1 Warm the oil in a frypan on low heat. Add the garlic, cook for a minute, then add the onions. Let 'em get golden (don't burn the stuff).

2 Dump in the tomatoes. Stir and cook for 10 minutes, uncovered. Add the cumin, oregano, salt, pepper and chili powder (you can always add more later — don't get it *too* hot!). Stir, add the stock, and stir again.

3 Mix and cook for 5 minutes

and throw in the TVP. Mix and add the beans. Mix again and put a lid on. Cook for five minutes and then taste. More salt? More chili powder? It's up to you. *You're* the chef!

To Serve Dish it up in warm small bowls. Add some shredded low-fat cheddar cheese or cheese substitute and you've done it. Great *Chili Con "No" Carne!* (con means "with" and carne means "meat" in dragon-ese — also in Spanish!)

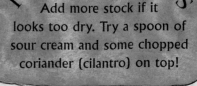

Herb's Hot Tips

Add more stock if it looks too dry. Try a spoon of sour cream and some chopped coriander (cilantro) on top!

That's **HOT!** But good and meaty!

I'm telling you, there's no meat in this chili.

EASY BURRITOS
Warm some flour tortillas in a pan for 5 seconds on each side. Fill with Chili Con "No" Carne and roll up. Top with cheese and sour cream.

Get your tongue into this one and join the *Gorse Chowder-Head Club*. He has his own cornfield and always brings over the first-picked ears and begs me to turn them into chowder. Hey, no big deal. You can do it too. Did you know that all dragons are corn-on-the-cob lovers? You don't believe me? Well, next time you have a dragon to dinner, serve him an ear (of corn!) and see what happens!

SLURP! Smells good.

Gee, a compliment!

Herb's Chowder for Chowder-Heads

▶ Here's what you'll have to hunt up: (Serves 6)

8 ears of fresh corn
½ onion, chopped fine
2 tablespoons butter
Some low-fat or regular milk (about 2-3 cups)
2 tomatoes, seeded and chopped
2 tablespoons chopped coriander

A bunch of fresh chives
1 lime, cut in four pieces
Spices: **¼ teaspoon each of:**
   ground cumin
   hot chili powder
   ground ginger
   ground coriander seed
   black pepper

Preparation time: 20 minutes

1 Boil the corn for 4 minutes, drain and cool. Cut off the kernels from 5 ears and put them in a blender. Add enough milk to cover corn and whizz for 1 minute.

2 Put the chopped onion in a small pan with butter and cook slowly until the onion is softened. Add to the blender.

3 Whizz for 30 seconds. Put the corn mix in a saucepot, add all the spices and stir.

Cooking time: 20 minutes

4 Add the whole kernels from the last 3 ears. Cook over a low heat, covered, for 5 minutes. Add milk to make it soupy.

To Serve Serve in warm bowls. Snip some chives over each with scissors. Add the chopped cold tomatoes and a squeeze of lime. It's a knock-out. (You can leave out or use less hot pepper, if you like.)

Gorse's Hot Tip

If you can't get fresh corn, frozen kernels will work — but don't use canned corn for this recipe.

THE STORY OF STONE SOUP

Grand-Pa-Pa-Snap-Dragon told me the story of Stone Soup. There are many versions but most tell the story of two travelers who stop at a poor village, light a fire, and begin to cook a stone in a pot of water. The villagers feel sorry for the homeless men and each offers a vegetable to add to the pot. A delicious soup is created because all have shared what little they had. I hunted up a fine, large stone and Grand-Pa-Pa shared *his* recipe with me.

Snap-Dragon's "Stone Soup"

▼ Here's what you'll have to hunt up: (Serves 6)

One clean, big stone
6 ounces (200gms) of tiny dried macaroni
1 pound (500gms) of borlotti (or similar) beans
A stalk of celery, peeled and chopped
2 small tomatoes, seeded and chopped
A small bunch of parsley, chopped

2 garlic cloves, pressed
1 large carrot, scraped and chopped
1/4 cup (60ml) olive oil and a splash
Bunch of fresh basil
Grated Parmesan cheese
Salt and pepper (to taste)
Dragon lake water (or tap!)

Preparation time: 20 minutes

1 Put the stone in a large saucepot. Add water to cover it by 3" (7cm). Boil for 1 minute. Add the beans, celery, parsley, tomatoes, splash of olive oil, garlic and carrot. Cook on a low heat for 30 minutes. Put a ladleful of soup in a blender and whizz for 10 seconds. Pour back into the pot. Add the salt and pepper. Cook for 10 minutes more.

2 Boil up the tiny pasta in lots of salted water. When it's

Cooking time: 45 minutes

cooked (not too soft!), drain it and add to the soup. If it looks too thick, add a bit of pasta cooking water so it's soupy.

3 Put the basil in a blender. Whizz for 10 seconds with 1/4 cup of olive oil and a teaspoon of salt.

To Serve Ladle the soup into warm bowls and dribble on some basil oil and a sprinkle of grated Parmesan cheese.

Is this one OK? It's my pet rock!

As long as it's bigger than your mouth!

Herb's Hot Tips

Boil *dried* beans in water for 10 minutes. Let them sit off the heat for 30 minutes. Drain and add to the main pot at Step 1.

GORSE GOES MEXICAN

My pal Gorse has this dead-easy way of making what he calls "Mexican Grilled Cheese Sandwiches." They're very tasty. He likes to cut them into quarters and spoon on *Herb's Radical Dragon Salsa*. I like 'em with a spicy tomato salsa, too. Of course, I know how to make tortillas from scratch, but you'll want to buy yours in a packet at the market. You'll see that I changed the name. More authentic!

Dragonian Quesadillas

▸ Here's what you'll have to hunt up: (Serves 2-4)

12 flour tortillas (tor-tee-yahs)
Monterey Jack Cheese (or cheddar)
Canola or peanut oil

FOR A SPICY TOMATO SALSA
2 cups (500ml) seeded and diced tomatoes

2 tablespoons diced red onion
Chili powder (to taste)
1 teaspoon salt
Juice of 1 lime
2 tablespoons chopped coriander
1 teaspoon cumin powder

Preparation time: 15 minutes   *Cooking time*: 12 minutes

1 Preheat the oven to 375°F (190°C; Gas #5). Lay six tortillas on a baking tray and cover with shredded cheese (as much as you like).

2 Cover each with a tortilla top, paint using a brush with a thin coat of the oil, and bake for 10-12 minutes until the tops are lightly browned and crisp.

3 *For the Spicy Tomato Salsa* Real easy: mix all of the stuff together in a bowl and let it stand for 5 minutes.

To Serve Cut each tortilla into quarters and serve with a bowl of the salsa on the side. Eat with your claws — whoops, I mean *fingers!*

How come you changed the name to Kay Sa Whatever?

Gorse's Hot Tips

For a fuller meal, add some cooked, sliced mushrooms along with the cheese and serve with *guacamole*.

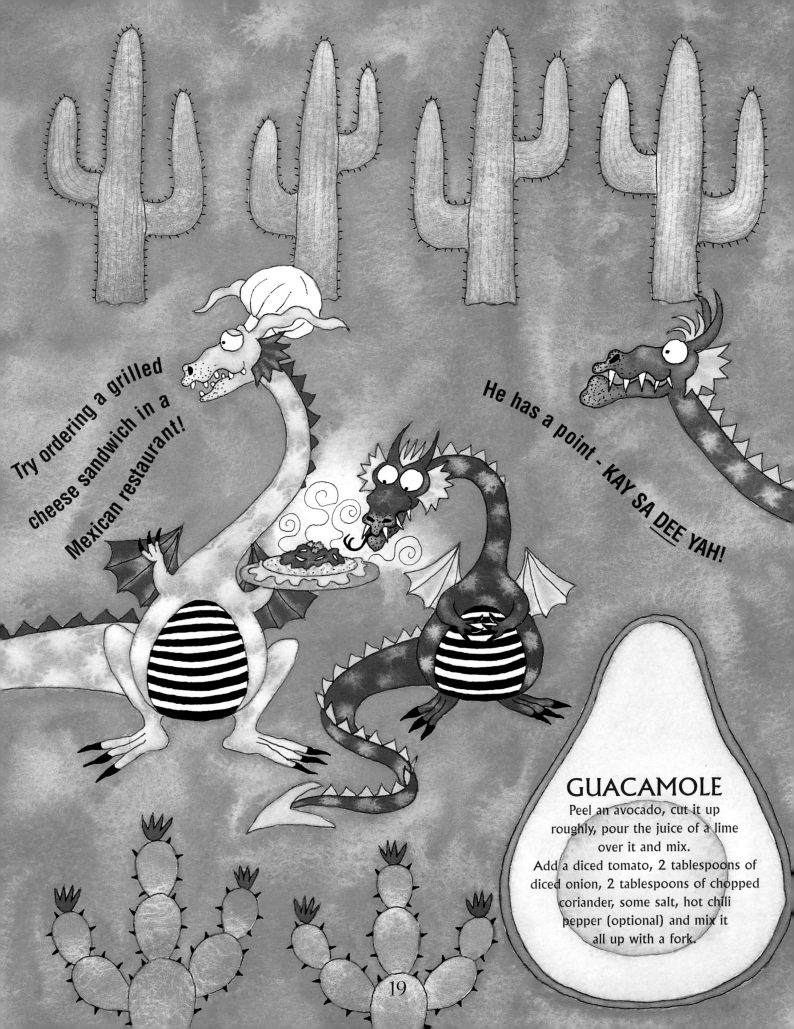

Try ordering a grilled cheese sandwich in a Mexican restaurant!

He has a point - KAY SA DEE YAH!

GUACAMOLE
Peel an avocado, cut it up roughly, pour the juice of a lime over it and mix.
Add a diced tomato, 2 tablespoons of diced onion, 2 tablespoons of chopped coriander, some salt, hot chili pepper (optional) and mix it all up with a fork.

I couldn't believe my ears when Meathook invited me to a dinner party for all his dragon pals — saying everyone was going to bring a dish. He asked me to prepare the MAIN COURSE and DESSERT...and would I bring some salad items from my garden? As he left he shouted, "Don't forget the salad dressing, Veggie-Head!" Something told me I was being taken advantage of, but never mind — he *did* invite me.

Party Pasta for a Herd of Dragons

But Herb had to cook <u>all</u> the food!

▾ Here's what you'll have to hunt up: (Serves 6 or 10 as a side dish)

You want MORE?

- 1 pound (450gm) of dried pasta shells (butterfly shapes are nice)
- 2 cups (500ml) cooked broccoli flowerets (see HOT TIPS)
- 4 tomatoes, chopped
- 12 sun-dried tomatoes (24 halves!) in oil, chopped
- 1 cup (250ml) fresh or defrosted peas
- 1 red onion, chopped fine
- 1 tablespoon dried oregano
- 2 tablespoons red vinegar
- 1/2 cup (125ml) olive oil
- 2 garlic cloves, squished
- Salt and pepper (to taste)
- About 12 fresh basil leaves

Preparation time: 25 minutes

Cooking time: 30 minutes

1 Fill a stockpot 2/3's with water and bring to a boil. Add one tablespoon of salt and the dried pasta. Taste at the 10-minute mark to see if it's done.

2 In a sauté pan or frypan add 1/4 cup (60ml) of olive oil and the garlic. Cook on low heat until the garlic is golden.

3 Drain the pasta in a colander, pour hot water over it and put it in a large bowl. Pour the olive oil and garlic mixture over it and mix. Add all the other ingredients and mix.

To Serve Tear up some basil and sprinkle it over as you sing your favorite song real loud!

Herb's Hot Tips
Do not refrigerate or the pasta will be gummy! Make broccoli and peas crunchy by boiling for two minutes ahead.

I discovered that there are entire books written about how to cook potatoes! Wow! Everyone has his or her favorite place to go for fries or chips, since they're best eaten out — you know where! So, let's forget about cooking them *that* way. My favorite recipe is really simple, but sometimes simple is best. I call them "amazing" because that's what everyone says when I serve them.

Herb's "Those Amazing Potatoes"

▸ Here's what you'll have to hunt up: (Serves 4)

4 large red-skinned potatoes
4 tablespoons olive oil

Salt and pepper (to taste)

Preparation time: 25 minutes

Cooking time: 20 minutes

1 Scrub the potatoes, then put them in a saucepot filled with water and boil for about 20 minutes until they are done *but still firm* (a knife should go through rather easily).

2 Put the potatoes in a colander and let them dry and cool.

3 Pre-heat the oven to 400ºF (205ºC; Gas #6). Put 1 tablespoon of olive oil in a baking dish. Slice the potatoes thickly and scatter (overlapping) in the dish. Pour the other 3 tablespoons of olive oil over the potatoes and add salt and pepper. Pop the dish into the oven.

4 *Peek in the oven from time to time*. When the slices are lightly golden in the center and browning around the edges, take them out.

To Serve Serve with veggie burgers or a mess of other vegetables.

I've had better. They're not THAT amazing.

You've eaten three portions!

Herb's Hot Tips
Don't peel the potatoes: the skins have lots of nutrients in them and are also very tasty.

Don't say "Who ever heard of a dragon who spoke French?" What language do you think dragons who live in France speak? Ever since Rosie-Rose learned to *par-lay fran-say*, she's been cooking French dishes. I love soup, so I asked her to make a French soup. Next day she swooped into my garden, made off with some leeks, onions, potatoes and chives, and left a note saying lunch was at 1pm. I was late, the soup got cold and Rosie was mad, but...

Zut! La soupe c'est froid!

Cold but good. Very good, Rosie.

Rosie-Rose's French "Cold" Potato Soup
because of Herb

▶ Here's what you'll have to hunt up: (Serves 4-6)

3 large potatoes, peeled and chunked
4 leeks (white part only), sliced
1 large onion, diced
6 cups (1500ml) water

2 cups (500ml) low-fat or regular milk
3 tablespoons sweet butter
Salt and pepper (to taste)
Bunch of fresh chives

Preparation time: 15 minutes

Cooking time: 30 minutes

1 Put a stock pot or large saucepot over a low heat and add the butter. As soon as it melts, add the leeks and onion. Put a lid on and let it cook for 5 minutes.

2 Add the potatoes and water and mix with a wooden spoon. Let it cook slowly on a low heat until the potatoes can be pierced easily with a fork.

3 Add salt and pepper and allow it to cool to room temperature.

4 Put the soup into a food processor or blender a little at a time and purée (which means to blend until smooth).

5 Pour into a pitcher or bowl. Mix in enough milk to make it soupy and leave in the refrigerator until cold.

To Serve Pour into bowls and snip chives over each. Even a kid can do it right the first time! *C'est facile!* (Say-fah-<u>seal</u>) which means: *It's easy!*

Rosie's French Tip
Try the French words:
Zut! La soupe c'est froid
Zoot! La-Soop-Say-Fwah
(Rats! The soup is cold)

THE DAY THE KING BECAME A VEGETARIAN

Boy, was I surprised to get a visit from the Royal Chef of the Kingdom of Nogard. "Herb," he said, "the King and Queen have decided to become vegetarians. Problem is, I know nothing about vegetarian cooking — so, I was hoping you'd give me a few recipes to replace the King's favorite, *Wild Boar-Burgers*. I tried a veggie version yesterday and the Royal Taster spit it out! I'm in big trouble, Herb." I think the recipe I gave him saved his *neck*!

The King's Favorite Veggie-Burger

▼ Here's what you'll have to hunt up: (Makes 4)

1 cup (250ml) fine textured vegetable protein (TVP)
1 carrot, scraped
1 large mushroom, chopped
1 small onion, chopped
1/2 small red sweet pepper, chopped roughly
1 garlic clove, squashed

Cooking-oil spray, and 1 tablespoon cooking oil
2 egg whites and 1 egg yolk
1/2 cup (125ml) breadcrumbs
1 cup (250ml) hot water
Salt and pepper (to taste)
Hamburger buns and ketchup

Preparation time: 25 minutes

Cooking time: 12 minutes

1 In a food processor, shred one carrot. Put a knife attachment in the processor bowl and add the mushroom, onion and pepper. Turn on the machine and run it until the mixture's all ground up.

2 Pour 2 tablespoons of cooking oil into a saucepot. Add the garlic and cook on a low heat. Add the contents of the processor bowl. Add salt and pepper.

3 Cook for 10 minutes on a low heat, stirring every few minutes. Put the TVP in a small bowl and add the hot water. Stir and cover. Let it sit for 5 minutes.

4 Add the TVP to the saucepot and mix well. Take it off the heat and mix in the eggs and breadcrumbs. Let it cool. Form into 4 burgers and refrigerate for at least a half-hour.

5 Spray a nonstick frypan with cooking oil. Over a medium-high heat, cook the burgers for 5 minutes on each side.

To Serve On toasted buns, with ketchup.

TVP? What does that stand for?

The King's Hot Tips

I like my burgers with a slice of onion. To make it sweet, my chef soaks it in water and ice cubes for a half-hour.

24

EAT A BOAT THAT DOESN'T FLOAT

I was having a party and wanted to serve a mess of veggies in a fun way along with a pasta dish. I got the idea from my sailboat, the *S.S. Zucchini*. I made Grand-Ma-Ma-Flora's delicious *Veggie Ra-ta-too* and spooned it into scooped-out zucchini halves. When I cut out the sails, I put names on them with crayons. They tell everyone where to sit and look great, too. Try it!

Veggie Sailboats

▾ Here's what you'll have to hunt up: (Serves 4)

4 long fat zucchini
1 red pepper, chopped
1 onion, chopped
1 small eggplant, chopped
**2 tomatoes, seeded and
   chopped**
¹/₄ cup (50ml) bread crumbs
¹/₄ cup (50ml) grated cheese

1 tablespoon olive oil
**1 garlic clove (optional),
   pressed**
1 teaspoon oregano
Salt and pepper (to taste)
White paper
Wooden skewers

Preparation time: 30 minutes

Cooking time: 15 minutes

1 Cut all the zucchini in half lengthwise and scrape out the seeds with a spoon (they should now look like dugout canoes!).

2 Put the olive oil in a sauté pan. Add garlic and turn the heat to low. Cook for one minute and add the onion and pepper. Mix and cook for 5 minutes. Add the eggplant. Mix. Cook for 4 minutes. Add the tomatoes and oregano. Mix. Cook for 5 minutes.

3 Add salt and pepper and spoon into the zucchini "boats." Sprinkle the bread crumbs and

cheese over each and drizzle some extra olive oil over them.

4 Preheat the oven to 375°F (190°C; Gas #5). Place the boats in a baking dish and bake for 15 minutes or until lightly browned on top. If the boats have been refrigerated, allow them to come to room temperature before baking.

To Serve Make a sail by cutting out a large triangle from a piece of white paper. Fold it in half and tape it around a wooden skewer. Stick it in the boat where a sail should be.

Herb's Hot Tips

If you put the boats in the refrigerator before cooking them, be sure to cover them with some wax paper or foil.

When I make these fritters I have to remember to save some batter for myself. Gorse and Rosie-Rose can scarf 'em down as fast as I make them — slathered with maple or corn syrup or just plain. I know they're good because ol' Meathook (who can't boil water!) sent one of his dragon pals to ask for (*steal*) the recipe.

Herb's Crunchy Corn Fritters

▶ Here's what you'll have to hunt up: (Serves 4)

2¹/₂ cups (625ml) of corn kernels (frozen)
¹/₂ cup (125ml) self-rising flour

2 large eggs
Canola or peanut oil for frying
Salt and pepper (to taste)

Preparation time: 20 minutes

Cooking time: 15 minutes

1 Cook the frozen corn according to the package instructions. Don't cook canned corn. Put ²/₃'s of the corn in a blender and whizz for 15 seconds.

2 Add one whole egg and one yolk. Keep the other egg white in a bowl. Season the blender stuff with salt and pepper. Turn on the blender and add 1 tablespoon of oil, then add the flour slowly. This is your batter. Put it in a bowl and add the rest of the corn kernels.

3 Beat the egg white until it is fairly stiff and add to the batter, mixing in with a rubber spatula.

4 Add 1 cup (250ml) of oil to frypan and heat on medium until the oil is hot (but not smoking). Add the batter by tablespoonfuls — flatten them a bit — and fry on both sides until dark golden.

To Serve Drain on absorbent paper and serve. Don't forget the maple syrup! (I like to heat it up).

We need that recipe!

No way, meatbrain.

Herb's Hot Tips

Don't let the oil get so hot that it smokes, or your fritters will turn black. Add extra oil to the pan for the second batch.

THE WATERMILL AT NOGARD FOREST

The old millstones, turned only by the movement of water from a stream, grind all the flour the townspeople and we dragons use to make bread. The stones also grind Gorse's dried corn into a gritty corn-flour that cooks up into a dish called *polenta*. Grand-Ma-Ma-Flora taught Gorse to make it two different ways: as a creamy side-dish (instead of mashed potatoes) and also formed into circles which she fried. Yum!

Flora's Crispy Polenta Circles (Made with Gorse's corn)

▼ Here's what you'll have to hunt up: (Serves 6-8)

2 cups (500ml) polenta cornmeal flour
1 cup (250ml) corn kernels, fresh or frozen

1 tablespoon salt
6½ cups (1625ml) water
3 tablespoons cooking oil

Preparation time: 30 minutes

Cooking time: 10 minutes

1 Cook the fresh corn in boiling water for 4 minutes. Cook the frozen corn according to the package directions.

2 Put the water in a saucepot and bring to a boil. Add the salt. Slowly add the polenta in a thin stream while mixing with a wooden spoon. When it's all in, turn the heat down to low.

3 Keep mixing with the spoon until the polenta pulls away from the sides of the pot and is thick but still pourable (*see HOT TIPS*).

4 Mix in the corn kernels. Pour onto a board or cookie sheet and smooth with a wet spatula

to make it an inch (2cm) or so thick. Cool to room temperature.

5 Cut circles with a cookie-cutter about 3" (7cm) in diameter or so. You can put it in the fridge for a while at this point, or continue.

6 Put 3 tablespoons of cooking oil in a frypan over a medium heat and fry the circles until golden and crispy on each side (peek under!).

To Serve Put on warm plates. You can pour over some maple or corn syrup or a spoon of your favorite salsa (or *Herb's Radical Salsa* — see page 36)

Flora's Hot Tips

You can serve the polenta when **Step 3** is completed, adding a little milk to make it creamy like mashed potatoes.

29

DO DRAGONS EAT PIZZA?

Do you know where pizza was invented? Some say it started with Egyptian flat bread. Do you know what the Italian word *pizza* means? It's "pie." It started to be popular after the end of World War II when the idea was brought back by soldiers who had been in Italy. Do you know the first *dragon* to make a pizza? You got it! Ol' Herb. No one in the forest of Nogard had ever heard of it, 'till me! Hey, amaze your friends with all this dragon-scoop.

Herb's Original Rainbow Pizza
Sort-of

▸ Here's what you'll have to hunt up: (Serves 4)

1 packaged pizza dough crust
¹/₂ green sweet pepper
¹/₂ yellow sweet pepper
2 mushrooms (cremini, portobello or white)

1 large ripe tomato
1 cup (250ml) mozzarella cheese, sliced
2 tablespoons olive oil
1 teaspoon dried oregano
Salt and pepper (to taste)

Preparation time: 25 minutes

Cooking time: 15 minutes

1 Pre-heat the oven to 425°F (220°C; Gas #7) and prepare the dough according to the package directions.

2 Cut the peppers along the natural indentations and cut out the white ribs, discarding the seeds. Slice the two mushrooms. Cut the tomato in half, take out the seeds and cut again in chunks.

3 In a frypan add 3 tablespoons of olive oil and turn the heat to medium. Add all of the peppers and cook,

turning from time to time, until the peppers are softened.

4 Arrange the peppers, tomato and mushrooms on the pizza in a colorful way, alternating stripes or in circles. Scatter the mozzarella around, sprinkle with oregano, salt, pepper and the rest of the olive oil. Pop it in the oven and bake until the crust is golden and crisp.

To Serve If you don't know how to serve pizza, I'm not going to tell you!

Needs a touch more oregano.

Royal Taster

Herb's Hot Tips

Don't put too much stuff on the pizza or it will get soggy. Better to save the ingredients for pizza number 2.

So many people and dragons have begged (hah!) for my special salad dressing recipe that I've finally given in and am printing it here for the first time! (Are you lucky, or what?) You'll find the 'secret' in my HOT TIP at the end of the recipe. While I was at it, I thought I'd also give you a few hints about how to make up a decent salad — something you should know.

For a jar of your secret salad dressing, the king will appoint you "Dresser of the Royal Salad".

Salads and Sweet 'n' Sour Dressing

▼ Here's what you'll have to hunt up:

For the Salad Dressing
2 tablespoons good red vinegar
1 tablespoon liquid sugar (see HOT TIPS below)
A tiny bit of pressed garlic
$1/2$ teaspoon salt
10 grindings of pepper
10 tablespoons olive oil
Mix it all up with a whisk.

For the Salad
Mix up stuff you like from these lists:
GROUP A
Bibb lettuce
Romaine lettuce
Curly endive (chicory)

Radicchio
Lamb's tongue greens
Endive
Dandelion greens
Watercress

GROUP B
Tomatoes
Radishes
Avocado
Cucumber
Basil leaves
Very thin sliced red onion
Shredded sweet red pepper
Black olives
Shredded carrots
Cooked sliced beets

Preparation time: 15 minutes

Choose one or more ingredients from group A and group B and mix them together with enough salad dressing to coat everything — but don't make it soggy.

Herb's Hot Tips

The secret is liquid sugar. Make it by cooking a cup of sugar with a cup of white vinegar until the sugar dissolves.

Hey, when you're a seven-year-old dragon, you don't want to stand in front of a hot stove for a half-hour stirring a pot of rice. Not when all your friends are having a good time swimming in Nogard lake without you. Right? Don't cry, try making risotto (ree-<u>zoh</u>-tow), which is Italian for rice, *my way*. It's just baked rice. No big deal. You might like it!

Do I really have to stir this rice for a half-hour?

Herb's Risotto Without Tears

▼ Here's what you'll have to hunt up: (Serves 4-6)

1½ cups rice (Italian short or regular long)
2 tablespoons butter
2 tablespoons olive oil
1 onion, minced fine
1 red bell pepper, seeded and minced
1 small can Italian tomatoes

3 cups (1000ml) vegetable stock
¼ teaspoon turmeric
1 clove garlic, squished
½ cup (50ml) Parmesan cheese
2 tablespoons fresh basil
Salt and pepper

Preparation time: 30 minutes

Cooking time: 30 minutes

1 Put veggie stock and turmeric in a large pot to boil. Turn oven to 350°F (190°C; Gas #5). Toss the garlic, olive oil and butter in a large straight-sided 10" (25cm) sauté pan that can go in the oven. Cook on a low flame, stirring from time to time, for 2 minutes. Then add the onion and red pepper and mix. Cook for 5 minutes more. Add the chopped tomatoes and mix again.

2 Add the rice and stir with a wooden spoon until all the

grains are coated with the mix. Pour in the hot veggie stock, salt and pepper and mix. *Carefully* put the pan in the oven and bake for 20 minutes. Sprinkle on the Parmesan cheese and bake for 5 more minutes.

To Serve *Carefully* take the pan out of the oven — make sure you're wearing **oven mitts!** Put on a warmer and cover with a cotton dishtowel (*not* a lid!). Share out the risotto, giving everyone a sprinkle of chopped basil.

Stop crying and check out my cookbook, page 34.

Herb's Hot Tips

When you add the Parmesan cheese, you can also add some crisp-steamed veggies like broccoli or mushrooms.

Now, I've heard of sending flowers on Valentine's Day, but ones you can *eat*? That was a first for me. Rosie-Rose called them *Sweet Pepper Flowers* and they were pretty as a picture — with petals of red, green and yellow. I must say they were delicious. I grow the peppers (and the parsley) in my garden and I always have too much of both, so I was happy to learn a new way of using them.

Rosie-Rose's Sweet Pepper Flowers

▾ Here's what you'll have to hunt up: (Serves 4)

3 sweet peppers (red, yellow and green)
$\frac{1}{2}$ cup (125ml) white bread crumbs
4 tablespoons chopped fresh parsley

1 small bunch radishes
1 garlic clove, pressed (optional)
$\frac{1}{2}$ cup (125ml) olive oil
$\frac{1}{2}$ teaspoon salt

Preparation time: 25 minutes

Cooking time: 15 minutes

1 Cut the peppers open along their natural rib indentations. Each pepper should give you about 6-8 long slices. Remove any seeds and hard white parts.

2 Boil some water in a large saucepot $\frac{2}{3}$ full. When the water boils, lower the heat to medium and add all the pepper slices. Cook for 3 minutes and drain in your colander. Let them cool.

3 Mix all the other ingredients (except the radishes) to make a nice pasty mess and spoon

this equally among the slices of peppers.

4 Oil a baking sheet and place the peppers on it, filling side up. Bake in a preheated oven 375°F (190°C; Gas #5) for 15 minutes.

To Serve Place the peppers on a round plate, alternating the colors in a circle (like forming the petals of a daisy). Cut the radishes into thin slices and make a circle of them in the center of the flower. Serve at room temperature as a first course or side dish.

She loves me, she loves me not...

She loves me, she loves me not...

Rosie's Hot Tips

It's fun to draw your meals before you make them. I always do. Try it with some crayons and a piece of paper.

SALSA! SALSA! SALSA!

One day I decided to add a dollop of corn salsa to Grand-Ma-Ma-Flora's *Crispy Polenta Circles*. At first she and Gorse turned up their noses at this unheard of addition — but now they both love it! Hah! You know what the word *salsa* means? In Spanish it's the word for *sauce*!

Herb's Radical Dragon-Salsa

OLÉ!

► Here's what you'll have to hunt up:

3 ears of fresh (or frozen) corn
5 tablespoons olive oil
¼ cup (50ml) sun-dried tomatoes, chopped
1 tablespoon lime juice

2 tablespoons chopped coriander
Chili powder (optional — see HOT TIP)
Salt (to taste)

Preparation time: 15 minutes

1 Boil the fresh corn in for 4 minutes. Drain and cool. Cook the frozen corn according to the package directions.

2 Cut off the kernels and put them in a bowl. Add all the other stuff and mix it up good. That's all there is to it.

To Serve This salsa goes great with *Herb's Crunchy Corn Fritters*, *The King's Favorite Veggie-Burger*, and *Flora's Crispy Polenta Circles*. Or just with chips! Super! (More ideas in HOT TIPS)

Herb's Hot Tips

For really HOT salsa, add some hot chili powder. But go easy. Remember, you can make it hotter but it's hard to make it milder!

THE COOKIE DRAGON

One Sunday, I awoke to find a plate of chocolate chip cookies in front of my lair. They were delicious! Each week I found more. Who was leaving them? The next Sunday I hid in a tree. Soon, I saw a dark shadow. I pounced and held it tightly. "Who are you?" I gasped. "I'm the *cookie dragon*. Set me free!". "Only if you give me the cookie recipe," I said. He had no choice but to reveal it.

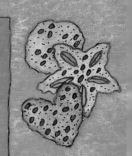

I think *YOU'RE* the Cookie Dragon.

Chocolate Chippers

▼ Here's what you'll have to hunt up: (Makes 24)

8 tablespoons canola/butter mix*

$^1/_3$ cup (75ml) granulated white sugar

$^1/_3$ cup (75ml) dark brown sugar

1 $^1/_3$ cups (325ml) all-purpose flour

1 egg

$^1/_2$ teaspoon salt

1 teaspoon vanilla extract

1 tablespoon dark molasses

$^1/_2$ teaspoon baking soda

1 cup (250ml) semi-sweet or milk-chocolate bits

$^1/_3$ cup (75ml) broken pecans (optional)

$^1/_4$ cup (50ml) raisins (if you like 'em — I do!)

(How did she guess????)

Preparation time: 25 minutes

Cooking time: 12 minutes

*To make Canola/Butter: in a bowl, allow 4 tablespoons of butter to come to room temperature. Add 4 tablespoons of oil. Whizz in a blender until combined. Scrape the mixture out into a bowl.

1 Preheat the oven to 375°F (190°C; Gas #5). Put all of the dry ingredients in a large bowl: flour, baking soda, sugars, salt, chocolate bits and broken pecans. Mix with a big spoon. Mix all of the wet ingredients in a small bowl: egg, vanilla, butter and molasses.

2 Dribble the wet stuff onto the dry stuff and mix with a spoon. You'll know you're done mixing when you can't see any more white flour in the bowl.

3 Put heaped tablespoons of the dough mix onto a non-stick baking tray, leaving some space between each cookie, and pat down lightly with your finger to make them somewhat round (neatness does *not* count!).

4 Slide them into the middle of the oven and bake for around 12 minutes.

To Serve Cool 'em, eat 'em. Make more!

Herb's Hot Tips

Why use the oil/butter mix? Because good eating habits start when you're young. It cuts down on butter and tastes great.

MEATHOOK'S BANANA GROVE

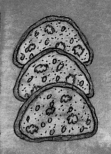

Bananas grew wild outside of Meathook's cave — but he never ate any of them. Each year they rotted. One day Rosie-Rose asked him if she could pick some. "Take 'em all," he growled. "I *hate* bananas." Rosie-Rose asked me what I could do with them and I came up with the bread recipe. Meathook smelled it baking and scarfed it down as fast as I could make it. Suddenly, he was a banana *lover*!

Keep 'em coming, Herb.

I thought you hated bananas?

Meathook's Favorite

Chocolate Banana Walnut Bread

▾ Here's what you'll have to hunt up:

$^1/_3$ cup (75ml) sugar	2 ripe bananas, fork mashed
4 tablespoons chocolate syrup	2 cups (500ml) flour
1 egg	1 tablespoon baking powder
4 tablespoons canola oil	$^1/_2$ teaspoon salt
$^1/_4$ cup (60ml) milk	12 walnut halves, broken up

Preparation time: 15 minutes

Cooking time: 1 hour

1 Preheat the oven to 350°F (180°C; Gas #4). Put the sugar, salt, egg, canola oil, milk and chocolate syrup in a bowl with an electric mixer. Mix until all is well blended. Add the fork-mashed bananas and mix again on medium speed until they're well blended in. Stop.

2 Add the flour, baking powder and walnuts to the bowl and mix again until no white flour shows and it's all thick and creamy.

3 With a rubber spatula, scrape the dough into a non-stick loaf-baking pan about 9" x 5" x 3" (23cm x 13cm x 8cm) that you have rubbed with a little bit of butter or oil.

4 Bake for 1 hour. Turn out and cool on a rack.

To Serve Cut into slices and place on a plate, overlapping like a fan.

Herb's Hot Tips

If you don't have a blender, you can make this by hand in a bowl with a wooden spoon and a whisk.

No one will believe you made it! Just tell 'em it's easy — when it's from Herb, the Vegetarian Dragon. Uh, maybe you'd best leave out the fact that I'm a dragon, unless your friends are very, you know, *advanced*? Hey, let me know how it turned out, okay? I think it's berry, berry good. Hah! If you have a better recipe, visit my personal website www.DragonHerb.com and send me an e-mail.

Herb's Simple Strawberry Slush

▾ Here's what you'll have to hunt up: (Serves 4)

2 cups (500ml) strawberries　　**1 cup (250ml) water**
²/₃ cup (150ml) sugar

Preparation time: Steps 1-3: 20 minutes + overnight freezing time
　　　　　　　　　Step 4: 5 minutes

1 Making simple syrup is easy! Slowly cook the sugar with the water in a saucepot until the sugar is dissolved. Boil it some more until you have only ²/₃ cup (150ml) (10-12 minutes) — and let it cool to room temperature before using.

2 Add the berries to a food processor fitted with a steel knife and pulse until the berries are chopped finely but not mushy!

3 Mix the berries and syrup in a glass bowl, then scrape into a plastic container with a lid.

Freeze overnight.

4 Set the bottom of the plastic container in hot water for a few seconds to loosen the slush. While still in the container, cut with a dull knife into small chunks and plop into the processor. Whizz for a minute or less, until it's a creamy frozen yummy glob. Scrape down the sides and whizz for another 5 seconds.

To Serve Spoon into chilled glasses and serve with a berry on top.

Come on, get cooking with Herb!

Herb's Hot Tips

Start and stop the food processor. Scrape down the sides. Start and stop again until it looks like frozen sorbet.

40

BAREFOOT BOOKS publishes high-quality picture books for
children of all ages and specializes in the work of artists and writers from
many cultures. If you have enjoyed this book and would like to receive a copy
of our current catalog, please contact our New York office —
Barefoot Books Inc., 37 West 17th Street, 4th Floor East,
New York, New York 10011
e-mail: ussales@barefoot-books.com   website: www.barefoot-books.com

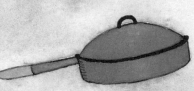